Leo the Late Bloomer

BY ROBERT KRAUS • PICTURES BY JOSE ARUEGO

Windmill Books
New York

Pub.

Published by Windmill Books, Inc.
257 Park Avenue South
New York, New York 10010
An Intext Publisher

FIRST PRINTING

ISBN 0-87807-042-7 Trade
ISBN 0-87807-043-5 Library
Library of Congress Catalog Card Number LC 70-159154

Manufactured in the United States of America
Published on the same day in Canada by Abelard-Schuman Canada Limited

For Ken Dewey

J. A.

For Pamela, Bruce
and Billy

R. K.

Leo couldn't do anything right.

He couldn't read.

He couldn't write.

He couldn't draw.

He was a sloppy eater.

And, he never said a word.

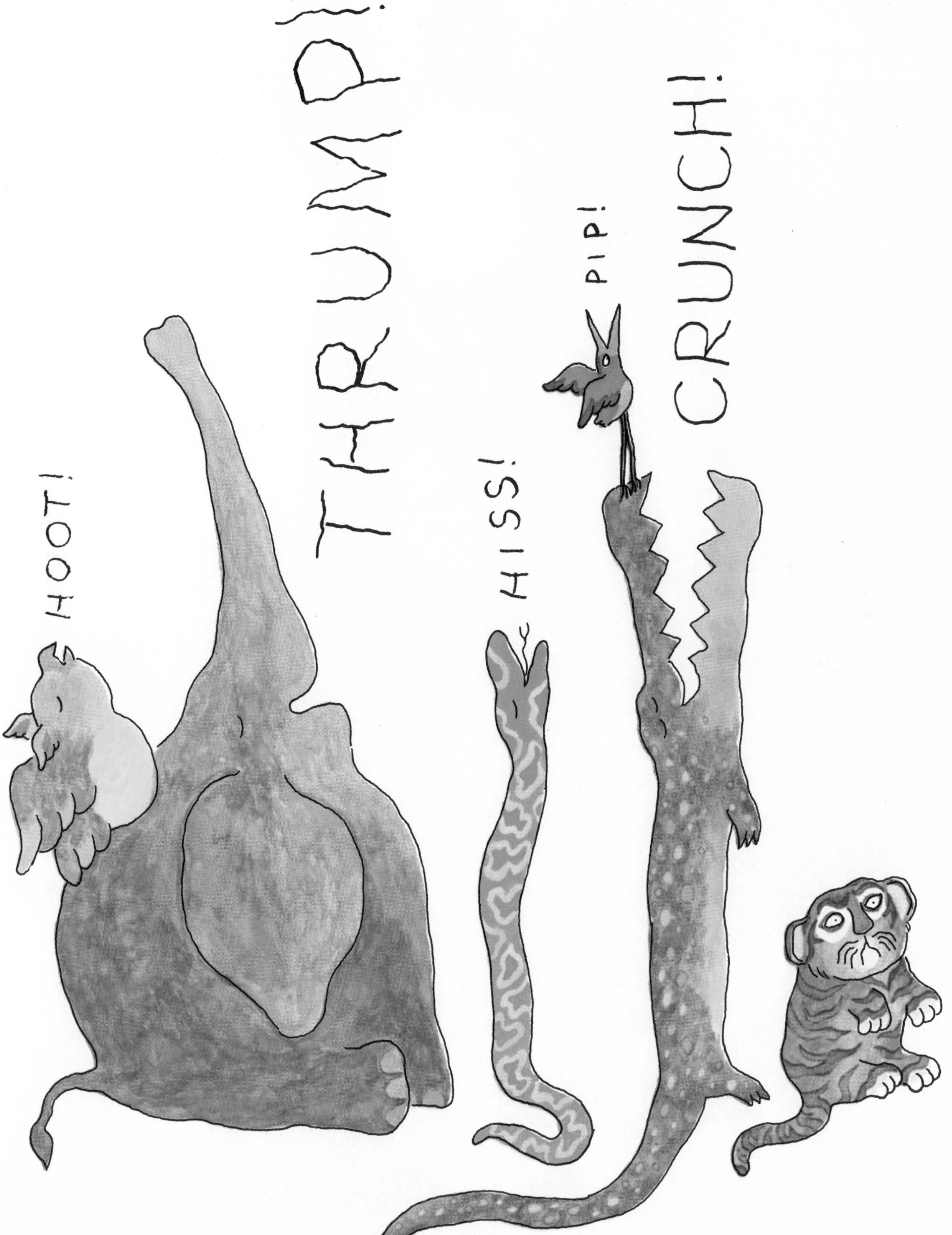

"What's the matter with Leo?"
asked Leo's father.
"Nothing," said Leo's mother.
"Leo is just a late bloomer."
"Better late than never," thought Leo's father.

Every day Leo's father watched him for signs of blooming.

And every night Leo's father watched him for signs of blooming.

"Are you sure Leo's a bloomer?"
asked Leo's father.
"Patience," said Leo's mother,
"A watched bloomer doesn't bloom."

So Leo's father watched television
instead of Leo.

The snows came.
Leo's father wasn't watching.
But Leo still wasn't blooming.

The trees budded.
Leo's father wasn't watching.
But Leo still wasn't blooming.

Then one day,
in his own good time,
Leo bloomed!

He could read!

He could write!

He could draw!

He ate neatly!

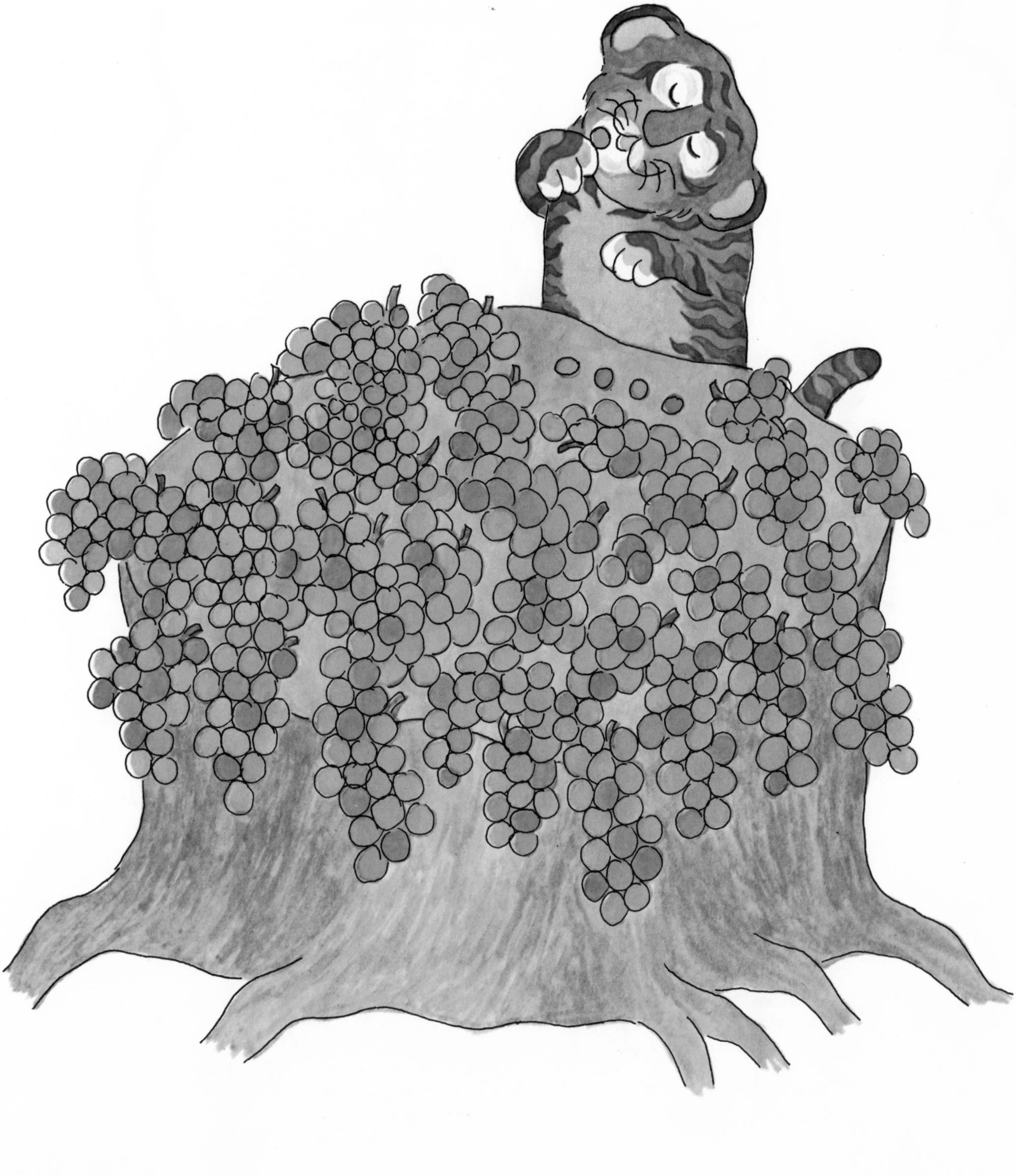

He also spoke.
And it wasn't just a word.
It was a whole sentence.
And that sentence was...

"I made it!"